D1010812

SOFIA MARTINEZ

Sofia's Party Shoes

by Jacqueline Jules

illustrated by Kim Smith

PICTURE WINDOW BOOKS
a capstone imprint

Sofia Martinez is published by
Picture Window Books, a Capstone imprint
1710 Roe Crest Drive
North Mankato, MN 56003
www.mycapstone.com

Library of Congress Cataloging-in-Publication Data
Names: Jules, Jacqueline, 1956– author. | Smith, Kim,
1986– illustrator.

Title: Sofia's party shoes / by Jacqueline Jules;
illustrated by Kim Smith.

Description: North Mankato, Minnesota : Picture
Window Books, a Capstone imprint, [2018] | Series:
Sofia Martinez | Includes Spanish words in the text,
a Spanish glossary, discussion questions, and writing
prompts.

Summary: Sofia has brand-new white shoes for
family friend Liliana's quinceañera, but when she
gets grape juice on them her mother makes her
wear them anyway, even though they no longer
match her white dress.

Identifiers: LCCN 2017039785 (print) | LCCN
2017042405 (ebook) | ISBN 9781515823384
(eBook PDF) | ISBN 9781515823360 (hardcover) |
ISBN9781515823421 (pbk.)

Subjects: LCSH: Quinceañera (Social custom)—
Juvenile fiction. | Hispanic Americans—Social life
and customs—Juvenile fiction. | Hispanic American
children—Juvenile fiction. | Hispanic American
families—Juvenile fiction. | Shoes—Juvenile
fiction. | CYAC: Quincea?nera (Social custom)—
Fiction. | Parties—Fiction. | Hispanic Americans—
Fiction. | Family life—Fiction. | Shoes—Fiction.

Classification: LCC PZ7.J92947 (ebook) | LCC PZ7.
J92947 So 2018 (print) | DDC [E]—dc23

Designer: Aruna Rangarajan
Art Director: Kay Fraser

Printed and bound in the United States of America.
010838S18

TABLE OF CONTENTS

CHAPTER 1

New Party Shoes

Sofia loved her new party shoes. They were white with lots of sparkle.

"They are very pretty," Sofia's older sister Elena said.

"Sí," Sofia's other sister Luisa agreed.

"Put the zapatos back in the box and in the closet," Mamá said. "They need to stay clean for the party tonight."

Tonight was their friend Liliana's quinceañera. The whole family was going.

Sofia was excited about going to a quinceañera. It was her first one! And she was really excited about wearing her new shoes. That made the party extra special.

Mamá, Elena, and Luisa left the room. Sofia planned to do what Mamá said. But she couldn't wait until tonight.

"I want to try them on one more time," Sofia decided.

She checked the hallway for Mamá. The hall was empty. Sofia went back to the closet and opened the box.

"Blanco," Sofia said. "Just like my party dress. A perfect match!"

Sofia's party dress had a ruffled white skirt. It was pretty, but it was not new.

Elena had worn the party dress first. Luisa had worn it too. Only the party shoes were Sofia's alone.

"I want to show my cousins," Sofia thought. "They are just across the backyard. Nothing will happen on such a short walk."

Sofia peeked into the hallway to check for Mamá again. It was clear! Sofia tiptoed down the stairs and out the door.

CHAPTER 2

Purple Juice

There was grass in the backyards between Sofia's house and her cousins' house. She looked down at her shoes. They sparkled in the sunlight. Would the green grass stain her shoes?

Sofia didn't want to take the chance. She took the long way around, using the sidewalk.

When she saw a melting purple lollipop, she hopped over it. She carefully stepped past a muddy puddle. And she slowly backed away from her neighbor's dog.

Sofia pointed at her feet. "Sorry, Bruno. I can't have dog slobber on me today."

Sofia arrived at her cousins' house with perfectly white shoes. Hector led her into the kitchen. Alonzo, Manuel, and baby Mariela were all drinking grape juice with Tía Carmen.

"¡Mira!" Sofia said. "My new party shoes!"

"Están muy bonitos," Tía Carmen said.

"¡Gracias!" Sofia said.

Baby Mariela waved her cup and dropped it from her high chair. It rolled near Sofia's feet.

The top on the baby cup kept the juice inside. Close call! Sofia's shoes were safe!

Alonzo leaned over for Mariela's
cup. As he did, his arm bumped
Manuel's juice. That cup didn't
have a lid. This time purple liquid
spilled all over!

Sofia tried to jump out of the
way. But it was too late.

"¡Qué pena!" Tía Carmen said.

"I'm so sorry," Alonzo said.

"It's not your fault," Sofia said.

"I should have listened to Mamá."

Tía Carmen scrubbed and scrubbed the shoes. Then Sofia scrubbed and scrubbed the shoes. But it was no use. The purple would not come off.

Sofia's new white party shoes were no longer white.

CHAPTER 3

The Party

Mamá shook her head when she saw Sofia's stained shoes. "You'll have to wear them like this."

"Yo sé," Sofia said.

When it was time to go to the party, Elena and Luisa got into the backseat of the car. They were all dressed up and smiling.

Sofia was frowning. Her arms were folded.

"Don't be grumpy," Mamá said. "You can still have a good time."

"Sí," Papá agreed. "A quinceañera is a celebration."

At the church, Sofia cheered up. It was exciting to see Liliana in her beautiful quinceañera gown. The long dress was sky blue with glittering beads.

"She looks like a princess!" Sofia told Mamá.

"¡Claro!" Mamá said. "This

is an important birthday for

Liliana. She is fifteen years old."

Before the special waltz, Liliana sat in a fancy chair. Her father helped her change from flat shoes into high heels. Her shoes matched her blue dress exactly.

Sofia looked down at her own party shoes. With all the purple spots, they didn't match her white dress anymore. Sofia sat down and took off her shoes.

"Oh, Sofia," Elena said. "It's not that bad."

"Join the party!" Luisa added.

Everyone was dancing a lot,
but it was uncomfortable dancing
in fancy dress shoes.

One by one the girls took off
their shoes, just like Sofia. By the
end of the night, there was a huge
pile of shoes.

"Are these mine?" Elena asked.

"No," another girl said.

"They're mine."

"All the shoes look alike!" Luisa complained.

"Not all of them!" Sofia said. She grabbed hers with a huge smile. "My shoes are easy to find!"

And that was the perfect way to end Sofia's first quinceañera.

Spanish Glossary

blanco — white

claro — of course

están muy bonitos — they are very pretty

gracias — thank you

mamá — Mom

mira — look

papá — Dad

qué pena — too bad

quinceañera — celebration of a girl's fifteenth birthday

sí — yes

tía — aunt

yo sé — I know

zapatos — shoes

Talk It Out

1. Were you surprised Sofia wore her new shoes before the party? Why or why not?

2. Do you think Sofia should have gotten in trouble for ruining her shoes? Why or why not?

3. Talk about a time when you took a bad situation and turned it into a good situation.

Write It Down

1. Pick three Spanish words from the story and use them in a short story.

2. Write a card to Liliana congratulating her on her special day.

3. Write about a time when you got something new. Be sure to include how you felt and why it was special.

About the Author

Jacqueline Jules is the award-winning author of more than forty children's books, including *No English* (2012 Forward National Literature Award), *Zapato Power: Freddie Ramos Takes Off* (2010 CYBILS Literary Award, Maryland Blue Crab Young Reader Honor Award, and ALSC Great Early Elementary Reads), and *Freddie Ramos Makes a Splash* (named on 2013 List of Best Children's Books of the Year by Bank Street College Committee).

When not reading, writing, or teaching, Jacqueline enjoys time with her family in northern Virginia.

About the Illustrator

Kim Smith has worked in magazines, advertising, animation, and children's gaming. She studied illustration at the Alberta College of Art and Design in Calgary, Alberta, where she now resides.

Kim is the illustrator of the middle-grade mystery series *The Ghost and Max Monroe*, the picture book *Over the River and Through the Woods*, and the cover of the middle-grade novel *How to Make a Million*.

FUN

doesn't stop here!

- Videos & Contests
- Games & Puzzles
- Friends & Favorites
- Authors & Illustrators

Discover more at
www.capstonekids.com

See you soon!

¡Nos vemos pronto!